To Evan, Tracy, Pete and Erin...

Karen

To Juliana Rue...

Vonnie

Published by Mouse! Publishing

P.O. Box 1674, Honolulu, Hawaii 96806

© 1994 Mouse! Publishing

ISBN: 0-9643512-0-X

Printed and bound in Hong Kong.

Keikilani,
The Kona Nightingale

Written by Vonnie Lyons

Illustrated by Karen Dougherty Spachner

MOUSE! PUBLISHING

HONOLULU, HAWAII

In Kona, on the Big Island of Hawaii,
donkeys live on a mountain overlooking
a place called Kona Village.
It is a beautiful mountain with
lots of wild grasses to eat.

Most Kona's donkeys bray (hee-haw) at night...which is a donkey's way of singing, but it isn't very pretty. A few special donkeys sing like birds. These donkeys are called Kona nightingales. A nightingale is a bird that sings beautiful songs at night. One of these special donkeys was Keikilani (Kay-kee-law-nee), which means child of heaven in Hawaiian. She was called Lani for short.

Lani was a good little girl. She loved her parents and they loved her. She was very happy and felt so good that all she wanted to do was play and have fun, but once in awhile she got into mischief.

Sometimes the donkeys would come down
off the mountain and cross the highway,
passing "Donkey Crossing" signs,
which warned drivers that donkeys may
be crossing the road. They would wander
toward Kona Village to drink rainwater
that collected in the rocks.

XING

The donkeys were not supposed to go to Kona Village because it was for people visiting Hawaii. It was clean and tidy and all the people who visited there were very happy. But, they probably would not have been too happy to have donkeys roaming around grazing off of the beautiful tropical plants and eating the grass.

One day, Lani decided to go to Kona Village. She knew that she wasn't supposed to go to there but it was on the ocean and she wanted to watch the boats and the swimmers. She especially wanted to get a closer look at the little thatched cottages. Lani didn't tell her parents she was going, she just trotted off down the trail.

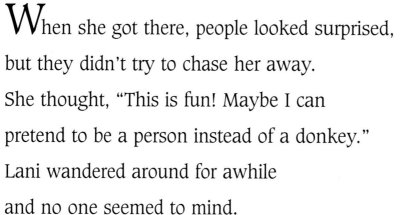

When she got there, people looked surprised, but they didn't try to chase her away. She thought, "This is fun! Maybe I can pretend to be a person instead of a donkey." Lani wandered around for awhile and no one seemed to mind.

She got up close to one of the thatched cottages and decided to nibble on the palm fronds that were used on the outside of the cottages to make the sides and roof. She was very hungry and they looked good.

All of a sudden a man came toward her.
It was Kainoa, the mayor of Kona Village.
"What do you think you are doing?", Kainoa roared.
"You can't eat our cottages and you don't belong here!
I'm going to take you to a farm where you can work
all day like donkeys should."

"No, no," Lani cried. "I'm not a working donkey. I'm special...I'm a Kona nightingale. I live with my family on the mountain and am free to do what I want. I just thought that Kona Village is so beautiful, and the people so friendly, that it would be a fun place to play and pretend that I was a person."

"Well, you're wrong, you're not free anymore," he said. "You're certainly not a person and besides you're eating up our cottages."

"Please let me go," Lani said. "If you do, I'll sing for you every night."

"You sing?," a surprised Kainoa asked.

"Yes," she said. "I'm a Kona nightingale and I can sing beautiful songs for you."

"Well," Kainoa said, "You really don't LOOK like a bad donkey... maybe you're just a bit playful."

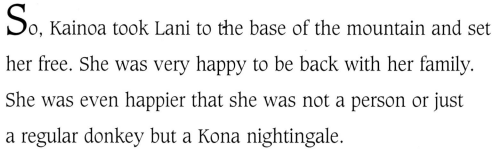

So, Kainoa took Lani to the base of the mountain and set her free. She was very happy to be back with her family. She was even happier that she was not a person or just a regular donkey but a Kona nightingale.

Best of all...Kainoa and Lani became good friends and now he lets her come to Kona Village whenever she wants... as long as she behaves herself!

Now, Lani sings to Kainoa every night...
and because he was so nice to set her free, she sings
a beautiful song that lulls him to sleep...a lullaby,
just like her parents sing to her.

And, sometimes she even falls
asleep herself after she finishes
her song. "Sweet dreams,
sweet dreams. Aloha and good night."